The
Peacock Garden
ANITA DESAI

Illustrated by
MEI-YIM LOW

MAMMOTH

For Rahul, Tani, Arjun and Kiran

First published in Great Britain 1979
by William Heinemann Ltd
Published 1991 by Mammoth
an imprint of Reed Consumer Books Limited
Michelin House, 81 Fulham Road, London SW3 6RB
and Auckland, Melbourne, Singapore and Toronto

Reprinted 1993 (twice)

Text copyright © Anita Desai 1979
Illustrations copyright © Mei-Yim Low 1991

ISBN 0 7497 0592 2

A CIP catalogue record for this title
is available from the British Library

Printed and bound in Great Britain
by Cox & Wyman Ltd, Reading, Berkshire

One

That summer, in 1947, the rains were late. Each day seemed hotter than the last in the little village in Punjal. The earth was scorched and every weed on it had withered. The water in the canals that criss-crossed the fields was all gone, and the clay lay cracked into smooth, pink tiles. The sky was yellow, the sun hidden by dust.

The nights, too, were so hot that it was difficult to sleep at all. As long ago as April, the family had moved its beds out into the courtyard for some cool night air. In May, they carried them up to the flat roof of their white house, to catch the few faint breezes that rose somewhere in the mango grove by the canal and murmured over the housetops.

In July, there were a few showers. The family had to wake up in the middle of the night, roll up their bedclothes and carry them down to the house and spread them out on the floor for the rest of the night. Zuni hated these nights, for it was stifling in the room with the small windows, and she wished she were allowed to stay out on the roof and feel the cool raindrops patter down on her hot, dry, dusty body. Her skin was covered with

5

prickly heat that was raw and red and itched terribly.

In August, the heat grew worse. Night after night, the family tossed and turned on their beds, getting up every now and then to drink from the earthen jar in a corner of the parapet that kept the water cool when the hot summer wind was blowing, but was now, on these airless, dull nights, warm and tasteless.

On the other rooftops, too, families were spread out on their cots. They could not sleep. Some sat in the faint starlight, playing their flutes. Some talked in low murmurs, in worried voices. Others paced the rooftops—white figures in the dark, slowly walking up and down, up and down, waiting for a breeze or a cloud—so Zuni thought. She knew they were waiting, but she did not really know what they were waiting for, nor did she know why they were so worried.

One night, when Zuni had fallen asleep very late out of sheer tiredness from tossing and turning on the burning hot bed, she was woken up by a heat worse than any she had known before, and voices—low and urgent close to her, but loud and wild in the distance where the bazaar was.

"What?" she cried, sitting up, feeling the heat burn her body, and then she saw flames leaping up to the sky in the neighbour's courtyard, like a huge bonfire. That was why she was so hot that perspiration was running down from under her hair, over her face, soaking her clothes. She cried out in fear.

Her father came immediately. He was a big man, with broad shoulders and a short black beard that had red streaks in it from henna dye. When he put his arm around her, she felt at once safe. But she was curious. "What's happened, Abba?" she cried. "Has Abdulla-*mia*'s house caught fire?"

"Yes," he whispered. "Speak softly, Zuni. Don't be afraid. I'll carry you away, but you must be quiet, quiet."

"Why? Why?" she cried softly, against his beard. "Why don't we go and help Abdulla-*mia*?"

"No, no, he's left—he's already gone," her father said, and Zuni could not understand at all why their neighbour had run away when his house had caught fire and not stayed to put it out.

She peeped over her father's shoulder at the fire as he carried her down the steep stairs to the courtyard, and then she was even more surprised to see her mother standing with her heavy black cloak right over her head, holding her sewing machine in her arms! What on earth was she doing with her sewing machine in the middle of the night? And behind her was Zuni's elder sister, Razia, also draped in her dark brown cloak and carrying a basket filled with pots and pans.

Zuni stretched out her arms to her mother. She cried "Amma!" She understood that they were running away, too—but why? Where to? And

1

why in the middle of the night?

"Shh!" someone hissed, and a dark figure slipped in through the narrow doorway of the courtyard. "Come," it called to them, "follow me—but in silence."

"Who's that?" Zuni whispered, clutching her father tightly about his neck.

"It is Gopal," Abba whispered. "He is taking us to a safe place. Now Zuni, no more talking. We must be silent," and he too slipped through the doorway, followed by Amma and Razia, each walking behind the other.

Gopal was the man who watched over Abba's mango grove down by the canal and helped to look after the cattle and take them to cattle fairs to trade. Gopal was not Muslim, like Abba's family, but a Hindu. That was why he could walk out in safety. Zuni could just make out his bald head and his white clothes, dim as a moth in the darkness. He carried no light. He led the way through the fields, between the bushes, along a very narrow path on which they kept stumbling. There was a faint sound of Amma's and Razia's cloaks as they swished through the dry grass and bushes, and a faint tinkling of the pots and pans that Razia carried in her basket. Everyone had his head bowed, and Zuni kept hers low on her father's shoulder, but she peeped back at the village.

She saw so many bonfires there now, not just one, immense ones with hungry blue and orange and scarlet flames reaching out into the hot, parched air. It was as if the whole village was on fire. Zuni could see that it was too big a fire to put out—there was so little water in the well these days, and none at all in the canals. That must be the reason why they were running away—but why in silence? Why in hiding? And she could hear voices in the village, at the end where the bazaar was, some screaming high, thin screams like kites battling in the sky, and some hoarse yelling. The voices sounded not only frightened, but mad, wild.

Zuni hid her face in her father's beard to keep from bursting with the questions in her that she had to keep still. His arms were strong and hard around her, but his feet often slipped and stumbled on the narrow, unlit path through the fields, and he was breathing hard. She felt the perspiration roll down his cheeks, into his beard and down his neck. Every now and then she peeped to see if Gopal was still in front, leading them, and if Amma and Razia were safely following. They kept close together in the dark.

Zuni heard the stray dogs of the village howling out in the fields, wailing as if they were in tears. Somewhere down by the canal bed a jackal answered, and its voice was even more sad and frightening. Now all they could see of the fire was the glow in the sky, angry and red.

Suddenly, white walls rose above them and

11

Gopal knocked lightly on a great wooden door. Then he put his mouth to a crack and whispered something that made the person at the other side very, very carefully open the door just a slit. Abba pressed through the narrow slit so that Zuni's legs scraped against the sides. Then Amma slipped through, struggling and panting with the heavy sewing machine, and then Razia, and immediately the door was shut behind them and bolted.

"But Gopal!" Zuni cried out aloud. "He's been left behind."

"It is safe for him outside," Abba said in a heavy voice, and he set Zuni down on the ground and straightened his back with a groan.

It was completely dark in that courtyard enclosed on all sides by white walls. There was not a single lamp lit anywhere. Nor did the wild glow of the fire reach them there.

Then the bent white figure that had so cautiously let them in whispered, "Come, I have a room for you." He led them over the tiled floor, opened another creaking, low door and let them into a small, close room that seemed to be full of straw

and stank of cattle. "You'll be safe here," he whispered and then shuffled away into the shadows.

Zuni felt her mother's hands on her head, then patting her cheeks with trembling fingers. "Lie down, Zuni," she whispered, "sleep now."

"Where, Amma?" Zuni cried. "I can't see any beds."

"In the straw, my dear," her mother replied and knelt to pat down the straw and spread her cloak on it to make a bed for her daughters.

That small, smelly, airless room was far hotter than their own room in the white house in the village. Zuni was sure it would be impossible to sleep. She lay down and the straw rose under the cloak and pricked her and scratched her in a hundred different places. She rolled over, bumped into the soft figure of her sister who lay curled up and trembling, and put her hand on Razia's arm, wishing to ask her something. But she couldn't remember what it was she wanted to ask, she was so tired, and then, strangely enough, she fell asleep instantly and soundly.

Two

Next day everything was made clear to Zuni.

She woke up to a low hum of talking, a confusion of cooking and washing sounds, and peeped out of the door, her dusty hair in wisps around her small white face from which the big, black eyes stared. She saw that the courtyard, that had seemed so dark and empty last night, was filled with people and their belongings in little bundles and sacks and baskets. She saw that the courtyard was lined on two sides with small rooms like theirs, and most of them were full of women and children, cooking, sleeping, sitting over their bundles and weeping, while the men stood about in the courtyard and talked. Abba was there, too, and a little bent figure in white who looked as though he might have been the one who had opened the door for them in the night.

Zuni looked back at Amma and Razia who were trying to light a small fire with sticks and straw and cook something in a pan. Both looked as dusty and ragged as Zuni, as if they had not slept or washed, and this surprised Zuni.

"Amma, what has happened? Who are they

all?" she whispered.

Her mother sat back and wiped her eyes, which were red with smoke, with the corner of the cloak she now wore over her shoulders, loosely, with straw still sticking out of its folds.

"Look out again, my dear," she said, very slowly, "and you will see that they are our neighbours from the village, and some from nearby villages. Our Muslim neighbours. We are the lucky ones who escaped from the fire and from the killers last night and are being sheltered here by the priests. No one will dare to kill us here in the mosque."

"Kill us?" Zuni cried out. "Who wants to kill us?"

"The Hindus, my dear. Kill us, or at least drive us away to Pakistan."

"What is that?"

"The new country for the Muslims across the border. The Hindus want us to leave India and go to Pakistan, to this new country."

Razia, sitting back from the fire, began to cry, whether because of the smoke in her eyes or for some other reason, Zuni could not make out. It worried her, for Razia was ten years older than her and she had not seen her cry before, so she pressed close to her sister and felt her shaking with sobs.

"Must we go?" Zuni asked, thinking that was the reason for Razia's sobs.

"If God wills it," Amma said. "Stop crying, my Razia, and help me clean these lentils and put them on. Abba will come with news soon—God willing," she said again.

Abba came in soon after, looking tired and careworn. He, too, was covered with dust and straw and his face looked lined.

"Have you found Ali?" Amma asked eagerly, holding the dripping spoon in one hand and quite forgetting about the lentils. "Or any of Ali's family?"

Ali was the young man whom Razia was to marry that winter. His family lived down the lane from them, in a yellow house with a balcony.

They owned a big grain store.

Abba shook his head and remained in the doorway, not sitting down. "No," he said, "they are not here. I hear they left in the night, by bullock-cart, for the border. They will be on their way to Pakistan."

Then Amma clapped her hand to her mouth, her eyes grew huge and dark as she stared at Razia, and she began to wail so loudly that Abba came in and hissed, "Stop, stop! No crying. No noise. We must expect such things at bad times like these. We should be happy they have escaped. They will soon be safe in Pakistan."

At that, Amma grew quieter—Abba always knew so well how to calm everyone, Zuni thought. Amma began to sound quite excited as she said, "Then we must go too. Let us escape as well. I've heard it said that trucks will come to take us to the Pakistan border with soldiers to protect us on the way."

But Abba, standing to his full height so that his head nearly touched the ceiling of the room, said very clearly and firmly, "No. There will be no running away for me. My land is here, my mango grove and my cattle. I have been talking to the priest here who says the Hindus will never attack a mosque. It is a place of worship and the Government of India has promised to protect it. It will be best to stay here till everything is quiet again and people become sensible once more and we can go back to our house."

Amma's mouth opened to let out a wail, but Abba gave her such a look, so strong and dark, that she said nothing at all. Razia dipped her head down onto her crossed arms and did not look up or say anything. Only Zuni still chattered.

"Will we stay here, Abba? In the mosque? When will we go home? Do you think the cattle will be all right? Will Gopal look after them?"

Abba just nodded but he took her hand and drew her out into the courtyard to meet the other families there.

Zuni, running through groups of refugees and

their bundles, soon found a bunch of her school-friends from the village. They saw her first and called, "Zuni!" so she dodged between the legs of the men who were standing around and talking and jumped over some rag-bag bundles and baskets and joined them, crying, "Amina! Zehra! Salima! Did you come here in the night too?"

"Yes, Chitra's father hid us on his bullock-cart under a pile of straw and brought us here."

"Hari's father helped us across the fields—he had a sword in his hand to kill anyone who tried to attack us. It was a very sharp sword—I touched it."

"Look, I brought my doll with me," Amina said. She was a pretty, pink-cheeked child of Zuni's age and she held up the little doll she had bought at the spring festival fair last year. Most of its paint was chipped off, but she was wrapped about in brightly printed rags that Amina had picked up in the tailor's shop that her father owned in the village.

"And see what I brought," Salima said, undoing a tight knot in a corner of her blue cloak and showing them the set of little clay fruit with which she liked to play—a tiny yellow banana, a small red pomegranate, some chipped yellow mangoes and a striped green watermelon.

Then Zuni, clapping her hands to her mouth, remembered the only toy she had ever had—a rag doll her mother had made her out of a roll of white

21

cloth with another, thinner roll stitched across it for arms. Amma had painted a smiling face on its head and sewn on two plaits of black wool. Razia had dressed it prettily for her. It was her only doll. She was called Mumtaz, and Zuni had left her behind.

She would have liked to cry, but of course, she could not do that in front of the other children. She swung around in a circle as though she were going to run home and fetch it, but she saw the high white walls of the courtyard all around her and, at the far end, the heavily barred and bolted wooden door.

"Shall we play house, Zuni?" the little girls asked her, spreading out their treasures on the packed clay earth under a spreading banyan tree.

But Zuni did not like to join them empty-handed. She was thinking about Mumtaz, lying tossed in a corner of their house—if the house was still there and not burnt to the ground, in which case Mumtaz was burnt to ashes too. "I have to go back to Amma," she said, and walked slowly away.

"Come and play, Zuni," Amina called again. "We're soon going away to Pakistan. Abba says big lorries are coming to fetch us and take us away."

Zuni wondered for a moment if it would not be more fun to travel to a brand-new country in a big lorry than stay here in this walled, locked courtyard. But then she thought again of Mumtaz lying alone in a corner, the big, brown-eyed cattle in her father's shed with their beautiful horns and the soft folds of their warm skin. The thought of the mango grove where she and Razia went to help pluck mangoes in summer and ate so many, sitting on the bank of the canal with their feet swinging in the green water as they sucked the sweet, orange flesh from the flat white seeds . . . and then she knew Abba had decided right and they should stay.

She wandered back to their small, stuffy room and found Amma and Razia sitting there alone, not caring to go out and talk to any of the other women. Both looked white, tired and sad as Zuni had never known them before. Usually they chattered to each other and laughed a lot as they cooked and sewed, but now they were silent. Zuni sat down beside them, feeling her head begin to throb from all the noise and heat and muddle.

"Amma, I left my Mumtaz behind," she said, pressing up against her mother like a puppy in need of comfort.

"Mumtaz?" murmured her mother as if she had never heard the name before.

"My doll, Amma," Zuni reminded her.

"The doll," Amma said, and shook her head as if she had other things to worry about. "We have left many things behind, Zuni," she said, and sighed so deeply that Zuni felt worse.

"When can we go back to the house, Amma?" Zuni asked.

"I don't know, child. No one knows. Abba says we must stay here till it is safe outside."

"But will they let us stay? Will the priest let us stay?"

Just then Abba came back to the room, bending down so that his head wouldn't bump against the low door. He heard Zuni's question and answered, "Yes, the priest has promised to let us have a house here—a better place than this room. I am to look after their cattle and their lemon trees and they will let us stay till we can go back in safety."

"And all the others?" Zuni asked, nodding at the humming crowds out in the courtyard.

"Most of them will be going by truck to Pakistan," Abba said. "They are waiting for the trucks to come."

Amma shifted suddenly and said, "Why can't we? Why should we not try, like them? It might be better . . ."

"How can it be better," Abba said with some anger, "when our land is here, not there? What is the good of going to a new country with empty hands? How will we eat? How will we live there?"

"But there may be nothing left here," Amma cried. "It may all be burnt!"

"Gopal promised to look after the house and cattle," Abba said. "God willing, he will be able to save them for us. He is a Hindu, he can stay on in the village and look after our things."

For a while Amma was quiet. Then she tried once more. "Ali will be there," she said, quite softly. "And Razia will be able to marry Ali there."

Abba turned and looked at Razia who sat in the darkest corner of the room, on a heap of straw, her arms crossed about her knees. "Razia," he said, but she did not answer. He reached out and touched her cheek gently. "Razia will wait," he said. "We are sure to hear from Ali again."

Razia cast her eyes down so that her lashes cast a shadow, dark as a moth, on her pale cheeks, and her lips trembled, but she did not cry. Amma, after watching her for a long time, suddenly whispered, "Look," and she went over to a corner

of the room where the sewing machine stood and lifted its wooden lid. She drew out something that shone and tinkled from it and Zuni jumped up to take a closer look. It was a heavy silver necklace of a beautiful mango design. Amma smiled as she turned it about in her hand, making it sparkle, and even Razia looked up.

"I told you not to bring anything valuable. What if we had been attacked on the way?" Abba said, sternly. "They would have killed us for that bit of silver."

But Amma smiled and said, "It is the necklace Razia will wear at her wedding. How could I leave it behind?"

Abba nodded as if he understood, but all he said was, "Aren't we going to eat today? Have you any food ready?"

So Amma quickly put the necklace back in its hiding place and started to stir the pot of lentils. But when she dished it out for them, Abba seemed not hungry after all and hardly ate. He had soon finished and sat in the doorway, staring out and thinking deeply.

The refugees in the courtyard of the mosque were getting worried because there was so little food left and it was not safe to go out for more. Then the trucks came at last to take them to Pakistan.

Zuni woke one night to hear the soldiers hammering at the door and making the old caretaker open it. All the men crowded about the door, armed with sticks and knives in case it was not the soldiers come to protect them, but the killers once again. But when the caretaker opened the door a crack, they saw the soldiers in their khaki uniforms, all stained with sweat, one of them holding a big torch in one hand and a sheet of paper in the other.

Abba and Zuni went out to watch, sleepy as they were.

"Are you all ready?" shouted the officer. "I will call out your name—step out and line up here. No big boxes allowed—only small bundles that you can carry yourselves. We haven't much space." The courtyard buzzed with life as if it were broad daylight instead of the middle of the night. The stars were covered with a blanket of dust and it was very dark. It was a wonder how fathers found their children, children their mothers, families their belongings. But in a short while they were all in a line with soldiers on either side of them to lead them out of the courtyard to the trucks that waited outside.

A few of them looked over their shoulders and called to Abba: "*Salaam Valeikum*, Habib-*mia*," and he called back in a hoarse voice, "*Valeikum Salaam!*"

Then they were all gone and the caretaker shut the heavy door and bolted it and only Abba and Zuni were left standing in the courtyard which suddenly seemed as bare and still as a graveyard. In the darkness, Zuni saw the white dome of the mosque rise above the treetops and walls, like a ghost. There was a sudden shriek that made her fly against Abba, crying, "What's that?"

It was the caretaker who answered as he shuffled off, tinkling the ring of keys tied to his side. "A peacock," he chuckled, "only a peacock." He went off towards his room in one corner of the courtyard, calling over his shoulder, "Tomorrow I'll show you your new home."

Abba lifted Zuni in his arms and called back, "We'll be ready for you in the morning." Then he hugged Zuni so that her face was pressed into his short, tickly beard and he said, "Sleep now. I'll hold you in my lap so you can sleep outdoors tonight. It's cooler here." He sat down by the doorway and was silent. He seemed to be listening for the sound of the trucks grinding up the dusty road towards Pakistan. But they could only hear the rustle of the banyan leaves and, sometimes, the sad cry of a peacock.

Three

When the old caretaker came for them in the morning, it was Abba who carried the heavy sewing machine, Razia had the basket of pots and pans again, and Amma tried to hold Zuni by the hand as they walked down the tiled courtyard which was littered with scraps left behind by the refugees. A thin yellow dog nosed amongst them. As they clattered across the tiles, a flock of parrots, as bright as leaves of young paddy, as bright as new mangoes or as gems, shot out of the old hairy grey banyan tree and fled, shrieking, into the hot white sky. Zuni was so excited that she pulled away from Amma and ran ahead, dancing at Abba's side.

They stopped beside the well from which all the refugees had drunk—a well as big as a small fort, with deep, dark sides and down at the very bottom, if you were bold enough to hang over the edge and look, a silent green pool of cool water in which frogs floated and plopped.

In the wall beside it was a small wooden door that Zuni had not noticed before, because the courtyard had been too crowded. Now the old caretaker opened it and Zuni sprang ahead of them all into another courtyard. This was not a tiled one with rooms all around it like the first. It was a huge garden, cut up into many small gardens, all a tangle of lemon trees, flowering creepers, mango and orange trees and patches of vegetables. The walls around it were low and of soft, grey stones. At the far end the rounded grey dome of an old tomb showed over the dusty leaves.

A brown hen and her chicks came rustling out of a mass of eggplants and gourd vines and Zuni ran after them in delight crying, "Chickens, Amma! Look, chickens!"

There were pigeons, too—she could hear them softly cooing in a big, leafy mango tree that grew beside a dripping tap. It seemed so much more shady and cool here than in the tiled courtyard.

"Come," Abba said, "we must not waste the good caretaker's time."

The caretaker stopped, parted some jasmine bushes over which a pumpkin vine had spread itself, and they saw the small, mud-walled, thatch-roofed hut in which he meant them to live.

It was as small and simple, just a little brown earthen thing with one room, as the very poorest people in the village lived in. It was nothing like the white-washed brick house the family had lived in.

Amma stood between two jasmine bushes, her hands pressed together, staring at it, and Razia stood at her side, looking as if she did not want to go into it.

But not Zuni. Zuni jumped when she saw it and darted past them all and ran up to the little hut, crying, "Is this our house, Abba? Oh, look, how pretty it is! What a tiny window. And there's a pigeon on the roof—perhaps it has its nest there. Look, Amma, a bush of chillies growing right beside the door! You can use them for cooking. Razia, see, the hen with the chicks is there under the bush—perhaps she lives here . . ."

Abba, listening to her chatter, began to laugh. He ducked his head and went in through the little door with the sewing machine. Then he peeped out of the window and said, "Come in, come in. What are you waiting for?"

Again it was Zuni who was the first to run in and admire the smooth clay floor and the wooden beams that held up the thatched roof and the coolness of the little hut.

It did not look as if Amma and Razia admired their new home as much. But they could not go on standing out in the sun so they came in and Amma set to work, unpacking the pots and pans and the few bits of bedding she had brought with her, spreading them out over the little room and making it look, if not like a proper home, then at least like a makeshift one.

"Well," she sighed as she tried to build a fire in the tiny stove made of two bricks and clay, "we are only refugees now."

Zuni said, "Amma, shall I bring you chillies from that bush?"

Abba smiled and pinched her cheek as she dashed past him. "I would like some chillies with my bread—nothing better," he said. "Then, if you can hurry up with the food, I'll go out and see what work they have for me."

So Amma had to hurry and, in a little while, that small earthen room, so dark and shady that one could hardly see, was filled with the good smell of fresh bread baked with chillies and onions, and the lentils she had cooked along with a ripe tomato Zuni had found on a bush outside.

"It seems Zuni is going to be our breadwinner," Abba said as he reached out for another helping.

"Oh, the garden is full of things to eat," Zuni said happily, "and full of things to see."

"Well, you can go out and explore later. Now it is too hot and you must lie down and rest."

Yet, when Zuni went out to explore the garden, the first thing she noticed was the grey stone wall that ran all around it and she could not help feeling shut in and a little frightened. She knew the open fields lay outside and would have liked to run out and see the farmers at work, the loaded bullock-carts go by and the children play in the mango groves, but the small wooden doors were all shut. And it was so quiet, too quiet for noisy Zuni.

As she stood there, wondering what she could

play all by herself, she saw flutter up onto the low wall a royal peacock, his breast a rich gold and blue and glittering green. She stood quite still by the lemon trees, gazing at him, and he sat just as still upon the grey stone wall, his lovely neck rising in an arch, his little golden crown quivering on his head, and his long tail, richer than any king's robe, trailing down the wall like a shower of jewels.

As Zuni watched, another bird flew up onto the wall, and another, and yet another—three peahens with only a glimmer of that gorgeous blue-gold, green-gold in their brown wings, and no lovely tail at all; his wives, all three of them. Then one seemed to spy something in the fields outside and flew off with a shriek. The others followed, all with these loud, sad shrieks of "Mee—o! Mee—o!"

At last Zuni dared move. She crept through the lemon trees and the tangled creepers of the vegetable garden where pumpkins, marrows and gourds grew all together, to the wall. She searched in the weeds, not minding the scratches she got on her hands and feet, till she found a peacock feather. It was like a round fan, made of rings of gold, green and blue, with a jewel for an eye in the centre.

She ran home and showed it to Amma who was scouring pots at the outdoor tap.

"Pretty," said Amma.

33

"The garden is full of peacocks, Amma," Zuni told her. "I saw four on the wall. One peacock and three peahens."

Her mother looked at her and smiled faintly. "But you have so often seen peacocks before, Zuni, in the fields. There were so many around our village, eating the grain."

"Yes, but these live here, in the garden—with us," Zuni explained. Stroking her cheek with the satiny feather, she went into the house and stuck it between a beam and the thatched roof. Razia was watching her so she told her, "I am going to collect peacock feathers and I'll cover the whole ceiling with them. Then, when we lie down, it will be like lying under the stars."

"Stars?" Razia laughed. "They don't look much like stars to me."

"Jewel-stars," said Zuni, and ran out.

Her search for peacock feathers led her all over the gardens around the mosque. She found that one walled garden opened into another walled garden, that one was full of lemon trees, another of loquat trees, that some had oleander bushes in bloom and others white jasmine. It no longer seemed closed and dull to her.

In one corner of the lemon orchard, she found a well and a cattle-shed where Abba was at work, feeding and watering the bullocks that lived there.

"Why do they keep bullocks, Abba?" she asked, patting the soft wrinkled neck of one that had mild brown eyes and did not turn its horns on her. "There are no fields here to plough."

"Their fields are just outside, Zuni," he said, fetching buckets of fodder for them. "They are usually busy in the fields outside, but now we cannot go out to look after the crops there."

"Why, Abba?" Zuni sat down on the edge of the well, swinging her legs and watching the bullocks snuffle into buckets of fodder and chew noisily.

"These are bad times—Hindus and Muslims, all have gone mad, they are killing each other and burning down houses and cities. The Hindus are driving Muslims out of India and Muslims are driving Hindus out of Pakistan. It is safer to stay here till everyone is calm again. We are quite safe here, inside the walls of the mosque."

"Oh yes, I know that," she assured him. She did not want him to think she was in the least bit afraid.

"Are you bored here, my Zuni, without any of your friends to play with?" he asked.

"No, Abba," she said. "I love this garden."

"Good," he said. "Now the sun is setting and I must go and say my prayers."

"Can I come with you?" she cried, springing down from the wall.

"Come," he said.

Hand in hand they walked through the garden of lemon trees, past their little hut that was quite hidden by bushes and creepers, through the doorway into the tiled courtyard where they had spent their first days here. The old caretaker in his little black prayer cap was hurrying towards the mosque in the centre of the courtyard. The parrots were screaming at each other from their holes in the trunks of the old banyan tree.

They walked down a narrow passage that was thickly covered by a creeper with large heart-shaped leaves and milky berries. Up the white marble stairs to the mosque they went—Abba setting his cap on his head and Zuni arranging her white cotton veil about hers. On feast days the mosque used to be crowded with men, kneeling and bowing and reciting their prayers, but now it was empty except for Abba, Zuni and the old priest.

Abba took Zuni by the hand over a floor as white and cool as iced milk, into a room where there were the tombs of a saint and his sons, spread with rich cloths of spangled silk and satin. Zuni felt dazzled by the splendid colours all around her. Above her were chandeliers of green and red and violet glass, hanging from a painted ceiling. On the floor were carpets as crimson as ripe plums, as scarlet as roses. On the walls were great fans made of peacock feathers and silver tinsel garlands with gold spangles. A tall, black-bearded priest, whom Zuni had not seen before was scattering rose petals and marigolds on the tombs. He was too busy to look up at them, but Zuni thought him stern and frightening.

Standing there by the door, she felt very brown and grubby and dusty. Suddenly, dust itched between the toes of her bare feet and she noticed that the veil she had wrapped about her head had a big hole in it. She felt so ashamed, she did not want to stay in that splendid room any more.

Abba was kneeling beside the tomb, saying a prayer, so she slipped out, and once she was in the cool, open veranda with its high arches, she felt happy and free again. The arches were like picture frames and through them she could see all the gardens and courtyards of the mosque and even over the low walls into the fields outside.

Zuni hugged one of the marble pillars of the arches and gazed and gazed—she had not seen the outside world for so long. She wondered if she could see their village and find out if their house still stood or was burnt down—but no, she couldn't. But there were the golden spires of the Sikh temple next door, gleaming in the evening light. And the open fields where she had played, and the mango groves, dark and leafy. The sun was setting, a large orange in the rosy sky. Just below the mosque, a peacock fluttered down from a loquat tree and vanished in the bushes.

"Zuni!" Abba called, and she ran to him.

"Are we going home?" she asked, beginning to feel hungry.

"No, I haven't said my prayers yet," he said. "I only went up there to pay my respects to the saint in whose honour this mosque has been built. After all, he is protecting us, isn't he?"

They went down the stairs to the big prayer hall with its marble arches and pillars and a ceiling painted with flowers. Here the tall priest was already kneeling and Abba quickly joined him. The old caretaker was mumbling in a corner by himself.

Zuni stayed outside and wandered about yet another courtyard, new to her. It was a graveyard, full of grey stone tombstones, and wandering amongst them was another royal peacock. It was strolling between the gravestones, now and then pecking at the ground, then raising its head to peep at her. She watched it till it disappeared in a grove of loquat trees.

Then she peeped down a hole in the ground into what seemed to be an underground cell. Her father found her there when he came out. "That's the underground cell where pilgrims would lock themselves up and pray for forgiveness for their sins. They would stay there for days without food or water or light, praying," he told her.

Zuni shuddered and slipped her hand into Abba's. "I would not be a pilgrim," she said. "I hate dark rooms."

"You are not a sinner," he laughed. "Now come, let us go home and see if Amma has found a lamp to light our house."

Four

Zuni's collection of peacock feathers grew fast and the ceiling of the thatched hut was spangled with their brilliant colours so that it really looked as though a rich cloth with a pattern of stars hung there. Zuni loved to lie on the cool clay floor, gazing up at them and listening to the breeze whisper in the dry straw. Somehow it made her feel cool and rested on the hottest afternoon. At night they slept outdoors, under real stars, and often heard the peacocks call, quite close to them. There was a sadness in their shrieks, but now they did not disturb Zuni—she knew them so well.

Although she was happy enough looking for their feathers under the lemon trees and watching the oranges slowly ripen as the days grew cooler, she sometimes wished she had a friend. How Amina would have loved to play house amongst the gravestones, and she and Zehra together would have fed the pigeons and the peacocks of the garden. Or if she just had her doll Mumtaz to talk to, in whispers, now and then. She even began to miss school. She had never much liked going there, sitting still and doing sums, but now she thought it would be better than being always alone in the silent, walled garden.

Razia had once laughed and played games with her—games with little round pebbles that they flung up in the air and caught on the backs of their hands, games played in squares and circles marked in the dust, games made up of little rhymes they had sung together. But now Razia was so silent and pale and sad that Zuni felt shy of her and kept away from her although she could see that Razia was just as lonely as she.

Amma sighed, "If only I had some cloth I could teach you to use the sewing machine, Razia—that would pass the time," but no one could go out to the market to buy cloth. Their grain and oil was brought to the doorway by some kind man whose face they never saw, and the vegetables they grew in the garden. Sometimes the brown hen laid an egg for them.

Then, one day, as Zuni was running down the courtyard to get a drink from the deep well, someone called to her from one of the small rooms around it. She stopped and walked back slowly to find an old lady with a white face, all wrapped up in a white cloak, peeping out at her.

"Come here, child," she called in a thin, weak voice. "I see you playing about all the time and you never come to see me."

Zuni went closer, very slowly. The old lady seemed ill for she was sitting up in bed.

"I am ill," she said, "and can't come out to visit your mother. Send her to me, will you?"

Zuni nodded quickly and turned and ran home to tell Amma at once. Amma seemed to know about her.

"She is the old caretaker's wife," she said. "Yes, we should go and see her. Come Razia, come Zuni, we can't sit moping by ourselves all the time. Let us go and visit the old lady."

The caretaker's wife seemed pleased to have visitors. She gave them sugared water to drink. It was rather warm water, but it had sugar in it and even a little rose scent and was the first sweet thing Zuni had had since coming to live here. She sat happily sipping her drink in a corner while Amma and Razia did the talking for once.

After that visit Zuni never went again, for fear of seeming greedy for more of that sweet drink, but Razia and Amma went often. They would take with them their basket of needles and thread and some scraps of old cloth that Amma found, and all sit together on the string bed, talking and embroidering. The old lady could embroider beautifully—she came from Lucknow where the famous embroidery is done on muslin—and Razia learnt eagerly and well.

"So we shall have a few things for your wedding after all," Amma said happily.

The nights grew too chilly for sleeping out and the family moved under the whispering thatch and the canopy of peacock feathers. The sun rose later out of a white mist that lay low on the ground and wrapped itself about the grey tombs and trees. The oranges were ripening on the trees. It was winter.

Zuni was sitting on the edge of the well, her chin in her hand, wondering what to do, when

Abba called her. "Come and help me pick oranges, Zuni. And ask Razia to come and help—if Amma doesn't need her."

Zuni jumped down and ran, she was so happy to be given something to do. To her surprise, Razia left the vegetables she was cutting up and jumped to her feet and followed Zuni out quite eagerly.

Abba was already busy under the trees, plucking the small ripe oranges into a big basket. He smiled at them. "With two daughters to help me, this won't take long," he said, and gave them each a basket.

It was harder work than Zuni had thought it would be, because although the trees were not

very tall, the oranges were often out of reach and they would have to climb up or drag down the branches to get all that were ripe. They were often scratched by thorns or sharp twigs and covered with the fine dust that slipped off the leaves. But they worked all morning.

At noon Amma came out to the orchard with a flat basket balanced on her head and a jar of cool water in one hand. She spread out their food under the flowering creeper that was like a great tent of bright orange flowers all winter, and then called Abba and the girls. They sat down under the bright flowers, in the winter sunshine, eating bread stuffed with radish and a potato curry Amma had made.

"It tastes wonderful, Amma," Zuni said, eating hungrily. "Can I have some more?"

Amma gave her another helping and then Razia asked for more, too. "If I had known eating outdoors would make you eat so well," said Amma, "I would have given you your meals outside every day."

"Perhaps you should do that," said Abba, taking a drink from the earthen jar.

Then they went back to plucking oranges and by late afternoon they had three baskets full to the brim with the small juicy oranges that left such a sweet smell on their fingers.

"What will we do with them, Abba?" asked Zuni.

"We will take them to the village tomorrow and sell them in the bazaar," he said, so quietly that for a minute Zuni didn't quite realize what he had said.

When she did, she gave a little jump of excitement then clapped her hand to her mouth in fright. "But Abba," she stammered, "how can we go to the village?"

"I think it will be safe now," Abba said. "The man who brings wheat and oil to the gate for us says it is all quiet there now and there is no more trouble. I have spoken to the priest and he thinks I should try and go back to the village. One day we will have to step out and start going about as we used to, so why not now?"

"Abba," Zuni burst out through her fingers, "can I go with you?"

He looked down at her small face and her big shining eyes. "Yes," he said, "I'll take you with me."

"Oh, Abba, when? What time?"

"Not now. Tomorrow morning. Come, let's go home. I would like to smoke my hookah now."

She danced all the way ahead of him, down the path that led through the trees to their hut, and while Abba settled down in the courtyard with his hookah, the water pipe that Razia had got ready for him, quietly bubbling at it, Zuni danced into the hut, singing, "Amma, we are going *out* tomorrow! Out, out, *out* into the village, Abba says."

49

Amma came hurrying out, wiping her hands on her skirts. "Is that true?" she asked breathlessly. "How can it be true? It can't be safe . . ."

"I am told it is safe," Abba said, "I believe the people who tell me so since they are good to me. Tomorrow Zuni and I will take the oranges to market. Tell me if there is anything I can buy you from there."

There were so many things that Amma needed very badly that she did not argue any more, but began to tell Abba all he could bring for her. Above all, she wanted news—news of their house, their cattle, their mango grove, Gopal, their neighbours, the whole village. "I want to hear everything," she said, and Abba promised to find out.

Five

The mist still lay white and chill about the walls and trees of the peacock garden when Abba, Zuni and the small boy who helped the old caretaker slipped out through the blue doorway into the road. They stood there for a few minutes—it seemed so strange to them to be on the outside of the grey stone walls that had protected them for so long. The road seemed very wide to them, and so open, so without protection. A little further up they could see the golden spires of the Sikh temple, shining in the early sunlight. Then a bus came roaring up the road in a great cloud of dust, honking its horn. Several milkmen came running through the fields with their milk pails clanking. They climbed onto the bus that took them to the city. It roared past the three figures standing still by the gate of the mosque with baskets of bright oranges.

"Come, let's go," Abba said at last, and they walked slowly, balancing the baskets on their heads.

Zuni found it all so strange—the dust under her feet, the brilliance of the white road in the morning light, the open fields stretching out on either side of her. She stayed close to Abba.

She could not tell why, but she was a little frightened and felt glad when they stepped off the road onto a narrow path that led through the sugar-cane fields. The tall canes, rustling in the breeze, were like green walls and protected her.

At last they came to their village. There it lay as peaceful, sunlit, and muddy as it had ever been. Zuni stood and stared, finding it hard to believe that it had been there all this time, unchanged, but Abba said, "Come along, Zuni, we'll go straight to the market-place," and she had to hurry to keep close to him.

Some women filling their brass pots at the water tap turned to stare at them. Some small children playing with marbles in the dust stopped and looked up as they passed. Then one of the women cried, "It is Habib-*mia* with Zuni!" and let her water pot fall with a great clatter and splash as she came running to greet them.

The other women hurried up too. "Habib-*mia*, where have you been?" they cried. Some of them, the mothers of Zuni's friends, Teta and Bina and Sundari, bent down and kissed her on the head, asking, "Where is Khalida? And Razia? Where have you been? We thought you had gone in the trucks to Pakistan . . ."

"No," Abba smiled at them. "How could I leave my village? My father planted the mango trees in

52

my grove, and his father was born here. We were always very close by—just there," and he pointed across the sugar-cane fields to the white dome of the mosque that rose like a sparkling white lotus above the fields and the trees. "We were quite safe in there all the time," he told them.

"No! And we never knew!" they said in amazement. "If only we had known, we would have come to see you."

Abba smiled at them and then went on down the narrow village lane to the market-place where he was recognized by the men. They came running to greet him, hugged him in their arms and questioned him. Again he told them their secret—how they had been living inside the walls of the mosque all along, safely and secretly.

At last he asked them, "And my house? What happened to my cattle? And to Gopal?"

Suddenly their voices fell, became sad and serious, and Zuni could not hear their answers. She was too busy whirling around and around, anyway, staring at the old familiar shops that ringed the market-place. There stood the barrow where peanuts were being roasted in clay pots of hot sand. In the corner was the sweet shop where steam was rising from the huge pans of creamy milk and flies were already clustering on the pyramids of sticky pink and green sweets. Next to it was the tailor's shop where the sewing machine rushed clattering over the bright, flowered cloth and little frilly mauve and yellow frocks swung from their hangers along the wall. It was so long since she had visited them.

Suddenly, Abba touched her shoulder. "Zuni, let's leave the oranges here. The boy will sell them for us. Would you like to visit your school?"

For the first time Zuni was so delighted by such a suggestion that she ran all the way to the small white-washed building just outside the market. She could hear the lessons in full swing—so many voices together reciting the multiplication tables. Suddenly she felt shy and hung back, clinging to Abba.

Abba pushed her towards the door gently and they peeped in. There was a sudden silence. Then the teacher, Zuni's old teacher with the grey whiskers and the spectacles tied up with strings, put down the ruler held in his hand and came hurrying towards them, saying, "Habib-*mia*! Zuni! Where have you come from? We thought you were in Pakistan!" and all the little girls jumped up from the cotton rugs on which they had been sitting cross-legged with their wooden writing tables, and rushed up to surround Zuni.

She saw their laughing brown faces all around her and the happiness and friendliness in their eyes and no longer felt shy.

"Zuni," Abba said, "I have to go over to see our house and the shed. I'll leave you here for a while."

"Can't I come?" Zuni whispered, remembering her doll Mumtaz and longing to see her old house.

But Abba said, "Not this time. I'll come back in a little while and fetch you."

The teacher took off his spectacles and said, "It is recess now. You may all play outside with Zuni till I ring the bell," and he smiled at them more kindly than he ever had before.

Out in the courtyard, in the centre of a group of girls—not so very large now that all the Muslim girls had gone and only the Hindu children were left—Zuni had to answer the many questions she was asked. She told them about the mosque, the peacocks and the orange and lemon trees. Then, holding Bina by both hands and swinging around till they both fell in a heap, she cried, "You must come and see it! Will you?"

"Oh yes," Bina cried, getting up with a jangle of glass bangles, and then the bell rang.

Zuni waited at the door for Abba to come as she did not know if he wanted her to join school again and the teacher, it seemed, did not know either. He let her sit on the doorstep while he made the girls recite a poem about a swing.

Abba came back quite soon. Before Zuni could ask any questions he said, "Come, we must go back to the market and see how the boy is doing with the oranges. Then we have to do all Amma's shopping, so walk fast—we must hurry." He strode on so fast that Zuni had to run to keep up with him and felt quite out of breath.

They found the boy by the peanut barrow. "I sold all the three baskets to the fruit-seller," he said proudly and gave Abba some rupee notes which Abba carefully folded and put away in his pocket to give to the caretaker later.

Then they visited one shop after the other and Zuni had a wonderful time helping Abba choose a new frying pan for Amma, a spoon with a long handle, packets of spices like cloves, coriander, cardamoms and cinnamon, a piece of blue cloth to make Razia a cloak that she would embroider, and some more for Amma to make into pillowcases.

Then Abba found he had a little money left over and, looking a little less hurried and stern, he took Zuni to the bangle-seller who sat cross-legged in the shade of the postbox, and asked her to choose six bangles for herself.

"Any colour?" she cried. "Oh Abba, perhaps red—no, the blue—no. Abba, may I buy a bag of peanuts instead? Or sweets, Abba?"

"All right," he laughed, "but first help me choose six for Razia and six for Amma," and they sat down on their heels beside the bangle-seller and chose watery-blue glass bangles for Razia and

red ones with gold flecks for Amma. The bangle-seller tied them with bits of red thread into two clinking, chiming bundles.

Then Zuni danced off to the peanut barrow and bought a bag full of hot roasted nuts with a delicious smell that tickled her nose so that it twitched like a rabbit's. While she was busy there, Abba went to the sweet-seller and bought some yellow *ladoos* in a little straw basket. Zuni gave a little squeal when she saw them—she loved *ladoos* better than any other sweets.

With all these packets and parcels tucked under their arms, or balanced on their heads, they set off down the path through the sugar-cane to the main road, and Zuni kept nibbling at her nuts so there were hardly any left by the time they crossed the road to the mosque.

Amma was waiting just at the other side of the door and, as soon as they had come in and the caretaker had bolted the door behind them, she cried, "Oh you are safe! Is it all peaceful now?"

"Quite peaceful," Abba said, handing over the parcels one by one, "and very friendly."

"And our house?" she cried. "And our cattle— did you see them?"

He looked at her and said softly, "The house is burnt, Khalida, and no one knows who ran away with the cattle. Gopal did his best, but the thieves had knives with them. They killed him and got away."

For a while they all stood shocked and silent to think the good Gopal had been killed while guarding their house and cattle. Zuni stopped eating nuts and blinked with tears. She did not bother now to ask what had happened to her doll Mumtaz.

"It is terrible," Amma whispered. "And the house—quite burnt?" She could not believe it was gone.

Abba nodded, then said, "Come, let us go in—I will tell you everything there."

But Amma stood holding the parcels and began to weep loudly, with tears running down her cheeks, so that the old caretaker's wife looked out from her open door and called, "It is God's will, Khalida, remember, God's will."

"And we are not homeless," Abba reminded her. "We have a house here now—a good place to live. We are safe and blessed by the saint here. We lead a good life in this garden, don't we, Zuni?"

Zuni had seen a peacock flutter down from the wall into the garden and she ran on, shouting, "I like it here, Abba, I like it better than the village." She saw Razia standing outside the hut, waiting for them, and called, "Look what we bought, Razia—bangles and *ladoos*! *Ladoos* and bangles!"

Six

Now the blue doorway was left open and Zuni could slip in and out as she chose. Every day that winter she walked to school and was happy to have so much to do and to be outdoors. On the way home she would pick up a stick of sugar-cane and chew it and suck its sugary juice. In the evenings, by the small charcoal fire, Razia helped her to do the lessons she had missed. The days were short and she had less time for playing in the orchard, looking for peacock feathers and visiting the mosque.

But one Sunday when she had climbed up the stairs to the marble parapet and looked through the beautiful arches at the fields, she saw that they were turning gold—the mustard was beginning to flower. Bright yellow flowers, the colour of spring.

As Zuni ran back through the gardens to tell Amma and Razia about the mustard blossoms, she heard a peacock shriek almost under her feet and stopped short. Then she saw an angry peahen scuttle across the path and disappear into a thick hedge, followed by one, two, three, four, five downy, plain brown chicks. She stood stock still under the loquat tree, listening to them cheeping to their mother who answered with short, scolding sounds as they rustled and scratched about in the weeds and dry leaves where Zuni could not see them.

When she got over her surprise, Zuni ran all the way to the cattle-shed where Abba was brushing down a new calf. It was just a few days old, still shaky on its fine, delicate legs, with long pinkish ears that had trouble standing up on its little soft head, hard at work trying to get milk from its mother. Zuni forgot about the mustard blossoms and told him about the peahen and its chicks.

"There must be many around now," Abba said. "It is the season for them. The farmers aren't as happy about them as you are—there'll be so many more peacocks to eat their grain. And these big birds really do eat a lot, you know."

"I'll feed them," Zuni promised. "I'll put some food out for the chicks under the loquat tree—I think that's where they live."

"You won't need to do that," Abba laughed. "Their mother will see to it they get enough to eat."

Zuni could hardly wait to go to school next day and tell the children about what she had seen. Sundari, who was growing quite jealous of Zuni who had so many beautiful secrets, said, "My hen has had chicks too—twelve of them, and our goat

62

has a new kid, brown as velvet."

But Teta and Bina thought the peahen's chicks would be more interesting and asked, "Couldn't we come and see them, Zuni? Can't we come and see your house and the peacock garden?"

"Of course!" Zuni answered. "Come, come."

"I never go to the mosque—I wouldn't go near it," Sundari sniffed.

But Teta and Bina ran home to their mothers after school and begged to be allowed to go home with Zuni. That afternoon the three girls ran all the way through the sugar-cane which was now being cut so there was only a patch left here and there, leaving the fields bare so they could look over them and see the mustard flowering under the bright blue sky, like a yellow veil drawn over the green fields. Last year Amma had dyed Zuni's veil yellow and she had worn it to the spring festival.

They slipped through the blue door quickly—it was the first time the two Hindu girls had been inside the walls of the mosque and they looked a little timid, as if they did not know quite what to expect. Zuni led them over the tiled courtyard, through the gate, down the path between the orange and loquat trees, to her small house. She looked a little timid, too, wondering what the girls would think of the single-roomed, thatched-roofed earthen hut. Well, they were sure to like the peacock feathers that covered the ceiling, she decided, and led them through the gap in the hedge.

But she could not take them in after all. The courtyard was full of visitors. Amma was sitting on the doorstep, smiling and talking quite gaily; Razia was just behind her, peeping out a bit shyly, and the visitors rested on rugs spread out on the clay floor of the courtyard, sipping sweet drinks and eating sliced guavas.

Zuni stopped in astonishment and Amma, seeing her, called, "Zuni, come. Look, friends from Pakistan have come to see us. They have come for the Id prayers. Come and say *Salaam Valeikum*."

Zuni bowed her head and touched her forehead politely with four fingers, peeping at the visitors as she did so. But they were not friends from the village. She did not know who they were, and felt shy. She turned and whispered to the girls, "Let's go and look for peacocks. Then we'll come back here later and I'll give you some guavas."

They spent the afternoon under the orange trees, looking for peacock feathers, and went to the cattle-shed to see the new calf.

"It is beautiful here, Zuni," Bina said, looking about her at the grey tomb all covered with the orange flowering creeper and at the dazzling white dome of the mosque rising above the walls and treetops. "Much more beautiful than the village."

"But we haven't seen the peahen and her

chicks," Teta grumbled.

Zuni was disappointed, too, about their not showing themselves to her friends. The sun was already dipping low over the golden mustard fields, a smoky orange ball, and the girls had to start for home before it grew dark.

Then, as they walked back down the path under the branches of the loquat tree, they heard a rustle, a scratching and a peeping. Zuni knelt down and parted the leaves of the hedge very, very quietly. The two girls knelt down beside her and peeped through the gap she had made amongst the leaves. There, in the shadows, they saw the peahen and her brood snuggling down together in a soft brown huddle for the night.

Teta wanted to shout and startle them so they would come out and show themselves. But Zuni would not let her. "They are sleeping now—you mustn't disturb them," she said. "Let's go into the house now and I'll give you some of my peacock feathers."

She took them home and found the visitors all gone, Amma and Razia sitting by themselves on the rugs, chattering and laughing together as they used to do in the old days. When Amma saw Zuni's friends she cried, "Bina! Teta! You have come at last. How are your mothers and sisters? Come, give me all the news of your families." Razia fetched them a plate of sliced guavas and Zuni went in and fetched them some peacock

feathers while they were talking to her mother.

Then it was almost dark and Bina jumped up saying, "We must run all the way home now, Teta—it's so late!" and they hurried down the path, Zuni ahead of them to show them the way to the blue door.

Just as they were about to step through the door that led to the tiled courtyard, they heard a loud shriek over their heads. Flying together in fright, the girls looked up and saw a large and magnificent peacock on the wall, arching its golden neck, fluttering its little crown and sweeping its beautiful blue tail like a king's train. Then another peacock cried out in answer and another, and a peacock and a peahen fluttered up onto the wall. The little girls stood in the shadows, holding hands and not making a sound, just staring with open mouths. They watched two more peacocks join these on the wall, and three peahens, looking like a court of kings and queens and noblemen, all dressed in silks and jewels for a great party. They bowed to each other and dipped their heads, then spread out their wings and fluttered them, and actually danced on their toes, up and down the length of the grey stone wall. After quite a long while, one of them fluttered down to the side of the well where splashes of water had made a pool on the stone tile, and drank from it. The others followed. They formed a ring about the pool, drinking, just like a ring of royal guests drinking round a table. They fluttered their tail feathers as though they were fans, and danced about the pool, now and then throwing back their heads and letting out loud calls.

The little girls stood pressed against each other in the doorway, holding their breaths, till at last the peacock party was over and, one by one, they flew away over the wall into the black leaves of the orchard.

Then the girls dared to move out of the shadows and, as they ran towards the blue gate, laughed with joy and said they had never seen a prettier sight. "It was just like a party," Teta said.

"Or a fair," cried Bina, slipping through the door.

"Come again, come again," Zuni called after them and stood watching them hurry home across the bare fields where the dry sugar-cane leaves were being burnt in great bonfires. As she walked back down the tiled courtyard, she saw that in some of the rooms that lined it, cooking fires had been lit and a few people were sitting outside the caretaker's door, talking. Wondering who they could be, she hurried home.

When she got back, Amma told her. Amma was sitting by the fire cooking her favourite pudding, *halwa*, her face glowing in the firelight. "They are pilgrims from Pakistan," she told Zuni. "The Indian Government lets them come to worship at the mosque on important festivals. They have come from Lahore, Zuni, and brought us a message from Ali." Then she looked across at Razia and they smiled at each other with a strange new joy. "Ali has sent a message, Zuni," she said, almost laughing with happiness. "Ali himself is coming, in just a few days. He will be here for Id. We shall celebrate Id together—and then there will be a wedding."

"But it will be too soon, Amma," Razia murmured worriedly.

"No, not too soon. I'll rush—I'll fly—you'll see how I manage," Amma promised. "And we'll have the wedding soon after Id. Zuni, Zuni, your sister is to be married!"

Zuni sat down beside them, not quite able to understand what was happening, but her eyes began to shine. She sniffed hungrily at the delicious *halwa* smell.

"You will have new clothes, Zuni," Amma said.

"I? I thought Razia must have them," Zuni said, surprised.

"Oh, Razia will have her bride's clothes—pink satin Abba must buy in the market for her skirt. A pink satin blouse and silver braid to line the veil—silver to match the necklace I have for you, Razia. And for you, my Zuni, what shall we buy? Shall we buy silk the colour of the peacock? Would you like to wear a skirt the colour of your darling peacock feathers? And gold to line your veil with? Shall we?" Amma laughed.

Zuni was so happy to hear her laugh, to see Razia smile, to think of herself in new clothes the colour of peacock feathers, that she could say nothing for once. Amma went on talking. "Yes, Zuni shall be a little peacock and dance at the wedding." She threw a handful of nuts and raisins into the pot of *halwa*. "Now run, call your father to come and eat while the *halwa* is hot," she said, and Zuni ran.

A SUDDEN PUFF OF GLITTERING SMOKE

Anne Fine

' "Not G-e-n-i-e! J-e-a-n-i-e!"
The Creature shrugged. "One little mistake," he said. "Even a genie gets rusty after five hundred years stuck in a ring." '

The disgruntled genie who appears on her desk seems to be the answer to Jeanie's problems – whatever she wishes, he will command. But Jeanie quickly discovers that she and her genie have very different views of the world.

A Sudden Puff of Glittering Smoke is the first part in Anne Fine's trilogy about a genie; followed by A Sudden Swirl of Icy Wind, the trilogy is concluded in A Sudden Glow of Gold.

Anne Fine is the winner of the Smarties Award (for Bill's New Frock) and the Carnegie Medal.

KAMLA AND KATE

Jamila Gavin

Kate is delighted when Kamla moves into her
street. At last she'll have someone to play with!
The two girls soon become best friends. They
learn about each other's way of life, and together
they get up to all kinds of mischief – like making
potato prints all over Kamla's bedroom wallpaper!

THREE INDIAN PRINCESSES
The stories of Savitri, Damayanti and Sita

Jamila Gavin

Savitri
Savitri leaves the palace to live with her husband in the jungle. She carries a dark secret. Satyvan will die within a year . . .

Damayanti
Everyone wishes to marry Princess Damayanti, even the gods. However, even the gods consent to the virtuous princess's marriage to King Nala . . . that is all except a demon who lays a curse on the couple.

Sita
Prince Rama is about to become king when he is banished by his jealous stepmother for 14 years. His wife, the loyal Sita, follows, but this is only the beginning of their suffering . . .

Three vibrant and powerful Indian folk-tales retold with great sensitivity and charm.

LISTEN TO THIS STORY –
Tales from the West Indies

Grace Hallworth

Brer Anansi and Brer Snake and *How trouble made the monkey eat pepper* are just two of the delightful stories included in this collection of West Indian folk tales. Grace Hallworth has retold them with all the humour and vitality of expression which she herself enjoyed so much as a child in Trinidad – and she has even contributed her own magical version of why the Kiskadee bird is so called. They are guaranteed to captivate children from a young age upwards.

SUMMER IN SMALL STREET

Geraldine Kaye

"What's funny about Small Street," said Ben, "is that all the houses are the same and all the people are different.

And that is what Ben likes best. There's Charlene and Leroy, who are determined to join in the carnival, and Tong who has a pet gecko, and Sharon whose Granny rides a motorbike, and Poppy who actually kicked the big fierce dinner lady, and of course their teacher, Mrs Robinson . . .

These warm and humorous stories about life in Small Street will be recognised and enjoyed by all children.

AKIMBO AND THE ELEPHANTS

Alexander McCall Smith

Akimbo knew he had to find the ivory poachers himself. Too many elephants were being killed and their babies left to die. Akimbo must save them. There was only one way – Akimbo had to become an elephant hunter himself.

The author is giving a percentage of his earnings from this book to ELEFRIENDS.

FILM BOY

Alexander McCall Smith

Prem loves films. Most of all he loves to watch Rasi Paliwar, his favourite film star. Rasi can run faster, jump higher and fight better than anyone else.

Prem can't believe his luck when Rasi himself visits the sweet stall where Prem works. But Rasi leaves too much money and Prem is determined to give it back. His honesty leads him first into trouble and then to a dream come true . . .

WILD ROBERT

Diana Wynne Jones

When the tourists invade the peace of Castlemaine, Heather escapes to the mound. People say it's the grave of Wild Robert, buried long ago with a box of treasure, but no-one really knows.

Heather is very unhappy: 'Wild Robert, I just wish you were really under there.'

A voice replied, 'Did somebody call?'

The most mischievous, handsome charmer comes back after 350 years to transform not only Heather's life but the tourists too . . .

A brilliant, funny and touching fantasy by an acclaimed storyteller.

A selected list of titles available from Mammoth

While every effort is made to keep prices low, it is sometimes necessary to increase prices at short notice. Mandarin Paperbacks reserves the right to show new retail prices on covers which may differ from those previously advertised in the text or elsewhere.

The prices shown below were correct at the time of going to press.

☐	7497 0366 0	**Dilly the Dinosaur**	Tony Bradman	£2.50
☐	7497 0137 4	**Flat Stanley**	Jeff Brown	£2.50
☐	7497 0306 7	**The Chocolate Touch**	P Skene Catling	£2.50
☐	7497 0568 X	**Dorrie and the Goblin**	Patricia Coombs	£2.50
☐	7497 0114 5	**Dear Grumble**	W J Corbett	£2.50
☐	7497 0054 8	**My Naughty Little Sister**	Dorothy Edwards	£2.50
☐	7497 0723 2	**The Little Prince (colour ed.)**	A Saint-Exupery	£3.99
☐	7497 0305 9	**Bill's New Frock**	Anne Fine	£2.99
☐	7497 0590 6	**Wild Robert**	Diana Wynne Jones	£2.50
☐	7497 0661 9	**The Six Bullerby Children**	Astrid Lindgren	£2.50
☐	7497 0319 9	**Dr Monsoon Taggert's Amazing Finishing Academy**	Andrew Matthews	£2.50
☐	7497 0420 9	**I Don't Want To!**	Bel Mooney	£2.50
☐	7497 0833 6	**Melanie and the Night Animal**	Gillian Rubinstein	£2.50
☐	7497 0264 8	**Akimbo and the Elephants**	A McCall Smith	£2.50
☐	7497 0048 3	**Friends and Brothers**	Dick King-Smith	£2.50
☐	7497 0795 X	**Owl Who Was Afraid of the Dark**	Jill Tomlinson	£2.99

All these books are available at your bookshop or newsagent, or can be ordered direct from the publisher. Just tick the titles you want and fill in the form below.

Mandarin Paperbacks, Cash Sales Department, PO Box 11, Falmouth, Cornwall TR10 9EN.

Please send cheque or postal order, no currency, for purchase price quoted and allow the following for postage and packing:

UK including BFPO	£1.00 for the first book, 50p for the second and 30p for each additional book ordered to a maximum charge of £3.00.
Overseas including Eire	£2 for the first book, £1.00 for the second and 50p for each additional book thereafter.

NAME (Block letters) ....

ADDRESS ....

....

☐ I enclose my remittance for ....

☐ I wish to pay by Access/Visa Card Number

Expiry Date